TUMBLE
BUNNIES

To my beloved Jennifer
M. H.

First edition 2005

Library of Congress Cataloging-in-Publication Data
Lasky, Kathryn.
Tumble bunnies / Kathryn Lasky ; illustrated by Marylin Hafner. —1st ed.
p. cm.
Summary: Feeling untalented in the team sports scheduled for his
school's Sports Spectacular, Clyde the rabbit develops his own event, a freestyle
tumbling routine with a dazzling move called the "twirly-burly."
ISBN 0-7636-2265-6
[1. Sports—Fiction. 2. Sportsmanship—Fiction. 3. Tumbling—Fiction.
4. Rabbits—Fiction.] I. Hafner, Marylin, ill. II. Title.
PZ7.L3274Tw 2005
[E]—dc22   2004052141

2 4 6 8 10 9 7 5 3 1

Printed in Singapore

This book was typeset in Sabon.
The illustrations were done in watercolor and ink.

Candlewick Press
2067 Massachusetts Avenue
Cambridge, Massachusetts 02140

visit us at www.candlewick.com

TUMBLE BUNNIES

KATHRYN LASKY illustrated by MARYLIN HAFNER

CANDLEWICK PRESS
CAMBRIDGE, MASSACHUSETTS

CLYDE WAS NERVOUS. The Sports Spectacular was a week away, and he knew he wouldn't be chosen for any team.

Not for the relay races, not for kickball, not for T-ball, not for the twenty-meter hop-a-thon. He was having that terrible left-out feeling already.

Clyde decided to try to improve his hops.

His older brother, Jefferson, shook his head. "Not with those spindly legs. Forget it, Clyde. And let's hope your gym shorts don't fall down."

"Gym shorts! I hate shorts."

Clyde closed his eyes and thought about the germs he could catch between now and next week. Just enough, he thought, to get sick but not real sick. Just sick enough to stay home.

"Clyde," his mother said, "you don't look very well. Why are you standing in the backyard with your eyes shut tight?"

"He's imagining how icky he's going to look in gym shorts for the Sports Spectacular."

"Nonsense. Clyde has handsome legs."

"Handsome legs!" Jefferson broke out laughing. "You want to see handsome legs? And they can jump! They can run!" Jefferson began whizzing around the yard. He leaped over a bush, jumped his dad's wheelbarrow, and then finished with a huge hop across his mom's tulips. "Born to hop!" he shouted.

Clyde, meanwhile, was trying to turn a cartwheel.

"Why, that's a lovely cartwheel, Clyde. Perfect form," his mother said.

"Cartwheeling's not a sport, Mom," Jefferson said. "He won't get on a team."

"Well, I don't know why not. It takes skill and precision."

Clyde grew sadder and sadder. When he went to bed, he tried not to think about the Sports Spectacular. And he especially tried not to think about teams being chosen.

That night, Clyde dreamed of a globe covered with people from every country on Earth, and maybe even a few Martians. Everyone was lined up because they were going to be chosen for teams. And every single human being on Earth and even the Martians were chosen except for Clyde. Clyde was left standing on a continent, on a planet in the middle of a universe all by himself—unchosen.

"I HATE TEAMS!" Clyde roared in his sleep.

The next morning, Clyde fiddled with his cereal and hardly ate a bite.

"Are you still worried about the teams, Clyde?" his mom asked.

"I'll never get on a team," Clyde mumbled.

"Teams mean everything," Jefferson said. "Teams are cool. I'm on the junior varsity T-ball team. More cereal, please."

"Well, you're on our team, Clyde. The home team!" his father boomed.

"Big deal," Jefferson said.

Clyde's mother's eyes narrowed to little slits. "I'll tell you what's going to be a big deal, Jefferson—when I keep you home from school for the Sports Spectacular because you're a miserable sport."

On his way to school, Clyde got a pebble in his shoe. "Ouch!" *That's it!* he thought, and he limped the rest of the way.

"What's happened to you?" asked his best friend, Rosemary, when she saw him.

"Just a sprain."

"You'll never get chosen with a bum leg," said Spike.

Clyde tried to look troubled. "Not even for T-ball?"

"Teams aren't everything, Spike," Rosemary said. "I myself plan to enter the freestyle acroballet event."

"Freestyle acroballet? What's that?" Clyde asked.

"Somersaults and pirouettes, arabesques and flips. I do it on the trampoline."

"Not with a team?" Clyde asked.

"Nope. There's only room for me on the trampoline."

"I've got a routine," Rosemary continued. "Mr. Bunnstein is helping me with my tumbling, and he says my routine is very individual. He says it expresses my natural grace and energy."

All morning, Clyde thought about what Rosemary had told him. Clyde drew a picture of himself turning a somersault. Then he drew one of himself on the trampoline, bouncing up high. Then he drew himself doing a jumping jack, and something that he made up called a twirly-burly.

Rosemary looked at the pictures. "That's neat, Clyde. Too bad about that limp, because this looks like a routine to me."

"A routine?" gasped Clyde. "I've got a routine?" Clyde's limp disappeared.

That night, Clyde climbed up onto his bed. He started bouncing. He did a jumping jack. "Cool!" He did a few somersaults, boinged off the bed, and landed squarely on his feet. "Hooray for spindly legs!" he said softly.

"Clyde!" his mother said. "What are you doing? Sounds as if the house is coming down."

"Twirly-burly! Watch this!" Clyde said, and whizzed in a spin off the bed. He landed perfectly.

"I call that the most dynamic tumbling ever!" exclaimed Clyde's dad.

The next day in school, Clyde told Rosemary about his routine.

They went together to see Mr. Bunnstein.

"Another freestyler, Mr. Bunnstein," Rosemary said.

"You doing acroballet, Clyde?"

"No, I'm doing . . ." Clyde hesitated. He wanted to think of a really cool name for what he was doing. Then he remembered what his father had said. "I am doing dynamic air tumbling."

"Wow!" Mr. Bunnstein and Rosemary both said.

"Okay, Clyde, just call me Coach and I'll help you."

"Okay, Coach!"

So Clyde showed Mr. Bunnstein his backward and forward somersaults and his twirly-burly. And Mr. Bunnstein taught him how to get more spin and go higher.

And every night, Clyde practiced on his bed and shook the whole house with his dynamic air tumbling.

Finally the big day arrived.

Mr. Bunnstein stood in the gym. "Welcome, boys and girls, to the Sports Spectacular. This year we have something special. The winners in each event will be able to participate in the All-City Games." A roar went up. "Now, those who wish to be on the T-ball teams, please line up over here." Clyde saw Jefferson race to where Mr. Bunnstein was pointing.

"Those who want to be on the kickball teams, over there." He pointed to the other side of the gym. "Captains, choose your players," he called out.

Rosemary leaned over to Clyde. "I hate teams," Rosemary whispered.

"Me too," said Clyde.

Clyde was beginning to worry about his routine. What if he went plop in the middle of his twirly-burly? What if his spindly legs just froze and he stood on the trampoline and couldn't move?

"All freestylers, please line up!" Mr. Bunnstein announced.

Clyde was surprised there were so many freestylers. He and Rosemary weren't the only ones who didn't like teams.

Fern was first on the balance beam. She walked down the beam, pranced, and then finished with a backward somersault.

"Amazing!" Clyde whispered.

"Good—but not much pizazz," said Rosemary.

Next it was Rosemary's turn. She stood perfectly still in the middle of the trampoline. Clyde held his breath. Suddenly she exploded into a fantastic leaping arabesque. She followed this with a series of tumbling somersaults and jumped up to do a pirouette. Just as she was coming down from the pirouette, Clyde saw a plop and heard a yelp.

"Oh no!" Clyde gasped, and dashed off the bench and up on the trampoline.

"My ankle," Rosemary groaned.

Mr. Bunnstein looked at it. "Just a sprain, dear. Let's get you to the nurse's office."

"I'll help," Clyde said.

"But Clyde, you're next," Rosemary said.

"It doesn't matter, Rosemary."

"We'll let him go later," Mr. Bunnstein said.

Soon Clyde was back. And now it was his turn.

He climbed up on the trampoline. Mr. Bunnstein gave him a wink. "Ready, Clyde?"

"Ready, Coach."

Clyde took a deep breath. He tried not to think about Rosemary. He started to jump. With each jump, he got higher. By the third jump, he was ready for the flying somersault.

Then he went into a set of jumping jacks, clapping his hands under his legs. "Wow!" he heard someone say. Now it was time for his twirly-burly. Clyde leaped into the air, spun around in an airborne blur, and landed perfectly.

Clyde finished. There was clapping. Almost as much as for Fern. He'd gotten through it. His shorts had stayed up, but his best friend . . . Then he heard the loudest hooray ever. He turned around and spotted Rosemary.

Mr. Bunnstein went to the microphone to announce the awards.

"The scores are just in for the T-ball games. The Blue team won eight to six against the Green team." Everyone clapped.

"And now in the freestyle events," Mr. Bunnstein announced. "The gold medal for most precisely performed routine on the balance beam goes to Fern." Everyone clapped.

"The award for best performance on the bars is a tie between Harry and Tommy."

Mr. Bunnstein called out the rest of the winners. All the medals were gone. Clyde hadn't won any. But someone was coming forward with a glowing light on the end of a stick.

"And finally"—Mr. Bunnstein paused—"the torch for the All-City Games is to be carried by the student who has performed with the most courage even in the face of great difficulties and who has shown the highest level of sportsmanship. . . .

"Clyde, will you please step forward and carry the torch!"

A huge cheer went up. Clyde suddenly became airborne.
And there wasn't even a trampoline!

That night, Clyde invited Rosemary over to celebrate.
He practiced carrying a candlestick and pretended it was
the torch for the All-City Games.

"Hey, Rosemary," Jefferson said. "Want to see my
pennant for winning?" He waved it in her face.

Rosemary blinked and took a bite of pizza. "Nice,"
she said.

When it was time for Rosemary to go home, Clyde helped her down the front walk to her mom's car.

"Rosemary, I've been thinking," Clyde said. "I've been thinking that there is one good thing about your sprained ankle."

"What?"

"If you hadn't sprained your ankle, I wouldn't have been able to show my courage in the face of great difficulties." Clyde paused. "And my sportsmanship. So I think it's only fair that you carry the torch with me."

Rosemary blinked. "Well, I've had great difficulties too, I guess."

"And you're a sport, Rosemary, a real sport."